ISBN 978-1-330-13166-4
PIBN 10033484

1 MONTH OF
FREE
READING

at

www.ForgottenBooks.com

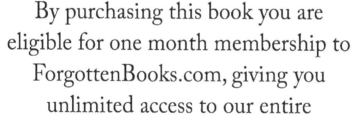

By purchasing this book you are eligible for one month membership to ForgottenBooks.com, giving you unlimited access to our entire collection of over 700,000 titles via our web site and mobile apps.

To claim your free month visit: www.forgottenbooks.com/free33484

English
Français
Deutsche
Italiano
Español
Português

www.forgottenbooks.com

Mythology Photography **Fiction**
Fishing Christianity **Art** Cooking
Essays Buddhism Freemasonry
Medicine **Biology** Music **Ancient**
Egypt Evolution Carpentry Physics
Dance Geology **Mathematics** Fitness
Shakespeare **Folklore** Yoga Marketing
Confidence Immortality Biographies
Poetry **Psychology** Witchcraft
Electronics Chemistry History **Law**
Accounting **Philosophy** Anthropology
Alchemy Drama Quantum Mechanics
Atheism Sexual Health **Ancient History**
Entrepreneurship Languages Sport
Paleontology Needlework Islam
Metaphysics Investment Archaeology
Parenting Statistics Criminology
Motivational

POEMS

—— BY ——

ALLEN PEABODY,

(BARD OF ENON.)

Who sent to Boston a petition
To make a law against folks fishing
Alwives out of Wenham water;
For he thought that no one ought to
Grag a seine or fish with line, or
Catch a pickerel, perch or shiner—
Only just himself.
Years have passed since Master John
Grew old, and died, and journeyed Home.
The little church, its ancient form and spire,
Its little bell would call to prayer or fire;
Its notes of joy, when July 4th came round,
Its solemn tones at funerals it would sound,
Is gone, and where it stood now stands an oval close,
Where shady trees and verdant grass now grows;
Where Parson Sperny preached for years and years,
Whose funeral sermons oft' drew briny tears.
Its sheep pen pews, whose rattling seats at prayer,
Made such a clatter every one would stare.
Its choir where Gould would sing, McCrea squeak and blow,
With clash of instruments made sacred music flow,
Might scare the angel from the house of God,
And rouse the dead asleep beneath the sod.
When Captain B —— would saw the cat gut bull,
And female windpipes make the clamor full.
Those days are past of fiddle, flute, bassoon,
And graceful organs made to take their room.
The church itself, was moved and filled with ice,
Where Heaven's wrath had threatened crime and vice,
Where hot discourses 'bout the realms below,
And Satan's dwelling where firey flames do glow.
Where Pluto reigns,—unpardoned sinners dwell,
And all the torments of an endless Hell;
'Tis fitting, 'tis, a gospel shop like this,
Should be hauled off and cooled with ice.
A modern church more comely in its style,

POEMS

BY

ALLEN PEABODY,

(BARD OF ENON.)

POEMS

—BY—

ALLEN PEABODY,

BARD OF ENON,

A HUMOROUS AND HISTORICAL COLLECTION.

GIVING THE JOKES, EXPERIENCES, AND

CHARACTERS OF MANY CITIZENS

OF WENHAM, 30 YEARS AGO,

AND PEOPLE OF THE

PRESENT TIME.

———————————

SALEM:

Steam Printing House of E. H. Fletcher & Co.

1868.

Fair Enon! What shall I about thee say?
Shall I go back to other days?
Shall I bring down from days of yore
The deeds of men, their names call o'er?
Their looks—their acts—and where they dwelt?
Their very names and how they're spelt?
Full fifty winters o'er my head,
Since I was born—have lightly sped;
'Tis four and thirty years ago,
Since first this place I came to know.
Since first I came to learn my trade,
St. Crispin's art, how shoes are made.
Then I was young—was scarce 18,—
Raw from the hills, untaught and green.
But long since then I came to know
Full many a joy and many a woe.
Accounts will interest you more
About your friends in days of yore;
Now Wenham Lake—then Wenham Pond;
Against it shores lived Master John;*
A Bachelor of much renown:
Well known by every one in town;
Who wore his trowsers in his boots,
Whose brains could figure squares and root,
Who loved to fish, and kept a boat,
But never knew the worth of soap;
Who sometimes kept the village school;
Taught A B C to dunce and fool;

*John Dodge.

Who sent to Boston a petition
To make a law against folks fishing
Alwives out of Wenham water;
For he thought that no one ought to
Grag a seine or fish with line, or
Catch a pickerel, perch or shiner—
Only just himself.
Years have passed since Master John
Grew old, and died, and journeyed Home.
The little church, its ancient form and spire,
Its little bell would call to prayer or fire;
Its notes of joy, when July 4th came round,
Its solemn tones at funerals it would sound,
Is gone, and where it stood now stands an oval close,
Where shady trees and verdant grass now grows;
Where Parson Sperny preached for years and years,
Whose funeral sermons oft' drew briny tears.
Its sheep pen pews, whose rattling seats at prayer,
Made such a clatter every one would stare.
Its choir where Gould would sing, McCrea squeak and blow,
With clash of instruments made sacred music flow,
Might scare the angel from the house of God,
And rouse the dead asleep beneath the sod.
When Captain B —— would saw the cat gut bull,
And female windpipes make the clamor full.
Those days are past of fiddle, flute, bassoon,
And graceful organs made to take their room.
The church itself, was moved and filled with ice,
Where Heaven's wrath had threatened crime and vice,
Where hot discourses 'bout the realms below,
And Satan's dwelling where firey flames do glow.
Where Pluto reigns,—unpardoned sinners dwell,
And all the torments of an endless Hell;
'Tis fitting, 'tis, a gospel shop like this,
Should be hauled off and cooled with ice.
A modern church more comely in its style,

Where gospel truths are preached in language mild,
To modern minds, improved by modern lore,
Where christian's meet to feast on Heaven's store.
There charity on brother christian's wait,
And honest meekness finds the narrow gate.
Oh let us hope the time is not far hence,
When prejudice will yield to common sense;
When bigotry will spend itself in lore,
And superstition be a thing of yore.

THE TWO TAVERNS.

In those old times two taverns stood,
Both upon the public road;
Ezra Lummus kept the one,
And Richard Dodge* and old Squire Thorne.
Richard Dodge sold rum, and dwelt
Where B. C. Putnam's house was built.
The well and pump is still in use,
Where man and beast may drink who choose.
Great improvements now have come,
Folks drink the water sans the rum;
But Ezra, farther up the town,
Where now the Essex road comes round.
The only dwelling built of brick, or
Where hay teamsters stopped to liquor;
Friend Ezra then kept grog for sale,
And thereby doth hang a tale.
For years and years, town meeting days
Were in excitement and amaze.
Full well do I remember how
The license question caused a row;
King Richard and King Alchohol
Kept tavern. and gave many a ball;
Where drunken rowdies met to prance,
Three cents for toddy, three for dance.

*This person's real name was John Thorn Dodge.

While Porter's Pompey tralled a reel,
And beat the measure with his heel,
Or Charley made his cat gut squeal.
Crazy Charley known to fame,
Charley Adams was his name.
Charley's history—I'll pursue,
His final fate none ever knew;
A few years later there was found
In Topsfield river some one drowned;
By some 'twas thought that Adams had
In stupor, met his end so sad.
Luke! don't you remember Luke,
Fat, hearty, jolly, like a Duke?
I've séen him dance an hour long
At Richard's—'mong the boozy throng.
When Pomp, or fiddle stopped the tune,
Roll like a cart wheel round the room;
Then swear and laugh, the jolly dog,
Three cents for musie—six for grog.
The "we sma'" hours of the night;
Found nearly all the party tight,
The moral people of the town,
On such proceedings used to frown.
The very ráts, folks used to say,
For very fear would skulk away;
For several days those frightened souls,
Would hardly dare to leave their holes.
The rotten beams of Richard's den,
Were tested well by drunken men;
Richard himself, I've heard it said,
In his bar room since fell dead.
Squire Thorn! at home town meeting days,
His voice for license he would raise,
Shrill above the noisy crowd,
His voice was heard in accents loud,
Saying, " Paul met three taverns and was glad,"

(His education sure was bad.)
Acts 28th, 15th verse,
Now read the text, where you of course
Will find, Paul *met* some friends and courage took,
This simple fact the Squire o'er looked.
Another " Old man eloquent,"
(Whose days on earth were nearly spent.)
This tumult, the Squire has raised the fuss,
'Minds me of Paul at Ephesus,
Whose preaching hurt the sale of gods,
The silversmiths deplored the odds.
Demetrius raised a hue and cry,
"Great is the god Diana."
The voters present saw the hit,
With loud huzzas applauded it;
"No license" was the vote they say,
And Dr. Killham won the day.

Three Selectmen.

One at the "Neck" one at "West End,"
Stephen Dodge and Peabody,
And Ezra Lummus made the three.
A committee had selected
These three men who were elected;
The first held to temperance views,
The third sold liquor when he chose.
One night a party met before
Our worthy townsman Lummus's door.
Rufus Dodge among the lot.
"Lummus how much rum 've you got?"
Says Lummus "Well, I rather guess,
'Bout eight gallons, more or less;"
Says Rufus "we'll pass round the hat,
Collect the chink and buy him out."
They let friend Ezra prize his rum,
They out with purse and raised the sum,

Then Rufus gave the bar a rap,
While with his hands he held his cap,
Now there's no game that two can't play it,
This is a fact although I say it.
Behind the counter stood some rum,
Drawn in a bowl which quickly come;
Friend Ezra turned it bottom up,
And Rufus caught it in his cap.
Old Alchohol was in the keg,
They brought him out—pulled out the peg,
And o'er the earth his blood did flow,
While his spirit went below;
And from that night until this minute,
This town has had no tavern in it.
With jolly Luke I have not done,
He was the talk of all the town.
How oft' I've seen his hand come down
On Israel Pert's unlucky crown;
Down Israel's cheeks the tears would run,
For quite one-sided was the fun.
Saying "Israel are ye wide awake?"
Then Luke would laugh just like a drake,
He'd then slap Israel on the back,
He laughed just as a duck would quack.
Poor Israel swearing all the while,
And people heard them half a mile.
Our neighbor Lummus had a colt,
And so one day fat Luke the dolt,
(Luke weighed at least three hundred pounds),
Got on this colt, and rode him round,
Though Dodge's Row and Wenham Neck,
His weight had well nigh broke his neck;
This is a new way, "Lummus swore,"
To break a colt, unknown before;
So Luke and Ezra had a spat,
And that's the last I heard of that.

I've seen him often on the house,
His voice would all the neighbors rouse,
And like a bugle he would blow,
And full a mile his voice would go,
O'er all the village it hath rung
From iron throat and brazen lung;
When all had heard him far and near,
His smutty head would disappear.
Luke died some dozen years ago,
But where he died I do not know,
And all in all he was a man,
Whose like we n'er shall see again.
Dr. Long was Dr. Dodge,
And Dr. Dodge was long,
I well remember Dr. Dodge,
And also Dr. Long,
Dr. Dodge was very tall,
And Dr. Long would stoop.
Dr. Appleton was poor,
Not in respect to wealth,
He had no flesh upon his bones,
He therefore had no health.
Peter Dodge sent for him,
For Peter's health was failing,
He felt the need of medicine,
Because he'd long been ailing.
And when the Dr's. carriage had come,
And the Dr's. horse had stopped,
Uncle Peter bluntly asked,
"Who dug this Doctor up."
Dodge was the tallest man in town,
About six feet and ten,
His head loomed up two feet
Above the average of men.
I oft' had seen him, walking home
From church on sabbath day,

He could look *down* on common folks,
And yet no pride display.
Dr. Jones another man,
Honest, brusque, and plain,
He never had an oily-tongue,
He falsehood did disdain.
These Doctors all were worthy men,
Jones likewise was tall,
Two Allen's next came on the stand,
I've named them nearly all.
Another Doctor, I'll yet name,
I do not doubt his skill,
He'll dose ye up to get well,
Or bleed ye if you will.
I would not like to *blow* him up,
He's played that game on *me*,
He left some *powders* at my house,
And skedaddled with his fee.
I am indebted to his skill,
He saved a precious life,
I now might sleep a widower,
Had he not saved my wife.
He *is* lightfingered, so look out,
I've often heard it said,
Pickpocket-like, this rogue would steal
Your teeth right out your head.
Jehu-like, you every day,
May see him driving round,
His popularity, has won
The practice of the town.
If you are sick just send him word,
His horse comes on the run,
He'll let you know your aches and ails,
Just like Jack Robinson.

AUNT THORN, (WIFE OF SQUIRE THORN DODGE.)

Old Aunt Thorn, kindhearted in the main,
Was not averse to trade and gain;
Bill Lakeman,* he could tell a tale,
How in old times he carried sail.
Thirty years ago I think,
Nearly every man would drink;
With many it became a passion,
And Billy Lakeman was in fashion.
Our hero, he got out of chink,
Was puzzled how to get a drink,
His genius struck a plan—t'was slicker,
By jingo, now I'll have some liquor.
He took a horse-shoe to the tavern bar,
And he found the lady there,
"I found this horse-shoe in the street,
I'll give it to you if you'll treat.
'Tis worth three cents, that's just the sum,
'Twill pay you for a glass of rum;"
He then passed it to the lady,
She mixed for him a glass of toddy.
She hung this horse-shoe on a rack,
He found a chance to steal it back;
So the next morn he called again,
"I've found *another* horse-shoe ma'm."
And so she traded as before,
And bought the horse-shoe back once more,
So every day he'd slyly come,
And steal *that* shoe to sell for rum.
One day he brought it to her door,
"I think I've seen *that* shoe before,"
She just began to smell "a mice,"
And Bill skedaddled in a trice.

*Mr. Lakeman is still living, and is now a steady, industrious and temperate townsman.

My hearers don't you be surprised,
Aunt Thorn was *often* victimized;.
She did not feed her boarders well,
If that be true I cannot tell.
T'was said Tom Wyatt boarded there,
And that he did not like his fare;
"I know a trick," thought Tommy Wyatt,
And blow me if I do not try it.
He caught a chicken, killed it dead,
He drove a pin into its head,
Then took this biddy to Aunt Thorn,
"I've found this pullet in the barn."
The simple lady thought it died,
"Go bury it," the woman cried.
"'Tis a pity," Tommy said,
"To bury it because it's dead."
"What is it good for," quoth Aunt Thorn,
"Since it died out in the barn?"
"Oh cook it granny, *I* can eat it,
Roast chicken's good, there'l nothing beat it."
Well, if you'll eat it then you may,
I'll have it cooked for you to-day.
Great country this! where poultry die,
Where I can dine on chicken pie,
Thought Wyatt when he came to dine,
I like this living it's so fine;
Great institution is a pin,
Guess I'll play that game again.
Aunt Thorn was useful in her day,
She had a sympathizing way;
If sickness called for extra care,
Aunt Dodge was sure to be there;
The pains of sickness she would ease,
The dainty appetite could please,
Her art would cool the fevered brow,
Very few knew better how.

Sit by the bed throughout the night,
And not depart till morning light;
Her sticks of candy won renown,
From grateful children in th' town.
Her faults were accidents of place,
She consequently bore disgrace;
The proud and selfish scorned her name,
Who never would have done the same.
Had they been asked to watch the bed,
And tend the sick or dress the dead,
Would have declined,—made an excuse,
In short would lie,—the truth abuse;
" I'm sick myself, or else *I'd* come,
Why don't you go and get Aunt Thorn."
What e'er her faults they must be small,
Her virtues overtopped them all,
She merited a worthy fame,
So let us all revere her name.

THE WRESTLERS.

There thirty years ago, was known
A wrestler who had n'er been thrown,
A man of famous nerve and strength,
Who made opponents gauge their length.
He was in fact a champion " crack,"
He had laid all Ipswich on its back,
And in pursuit of more renown,
He crossed the boundaries of his town.
March meeting day this blustering swell,
Came into town his deeds to tell,
With bragging gait he let folks know,
There was no man he could not throw.
Many confident, essayed,
Took hold to wrestle, but were laid,
People really 'gan to think,

What with muscle, what with drink}
That Devil Ben would rule the day,
And carry the champion's belt away.
So pride made many look around,
To find a man to put him down,
The terms of victory were known,
The man should treat who should be thrown,
At last the crowd produced a man,
Who said, "I'll do the best I can,",
The two took hold with iron grip,
Began to pull and jerk and trip;
The sweat began to ooze and run,
The gaping crowd enjoyed the fun.
With superhuman strength and tact,
He laid the bully on his back,
Then Devil Ben sprang up and swore,
"We'll try again, that was not fair."
Again he stretched upon the ground,
And all his boasting pride came down,
The champion's belt so people say,
Is by John Mildram worn to-day.

THE ORATOR.

Lummus had in his employ,
  Luke and Israel Pert,
Jo Pettingail and other men,
  At times were there at work.

These sons of vulcan loved a joke,
  At other folks expense,
Jack Newell was their victim once,
  And he lacked common sense;

They said he was a Cicero,
  Or modern Demosthenes,
That Clay and Webster did not know,
  How to distinguish beans.

That Newell could excell them all,
  If people only knew,
What an orator he was,
  Which *they* professed was true.

A hogshead full of water stood
  Just in that position,
Where an orator might stand,
  And deliver an oration.

They had a board cut half in two,
  To place above the liquor,
Just strong enough to bear a man;
  A half an inch or thicker.

They got the preacher on the stand,
  Stood by to hold it steady,
Thro' fear an accident might hap',
  " 'Twas high, he might be giddy."

And when the preacher spread himself
  In earnest declamation,
'Bout Washington and Bunker Hill
  And great men of the nation,—

Just then the crafty Luke
  Would the rostrum part asunder ;
His eloquence would then come down
  Kersplash and all go under.

The dripping orator would crawl
  Forthwith from out the water;
While Luke would roll upon the ground
  And shake himself with laughter.

THE LORD'S BREAD.

Old Richards used to peddle bread
  He bought of Mr. Lord;
When dealing with his customers,
  He'd pun upon the word.

He asked a wife in Topsfield once,
  If the Lord's bread she'd buy;
"Not when the devil peddles it,"
  Was the tart reply.

PELETIAH BROWN.

A party at a shooting once,
  Had took a chance all round,—
The turkey still alive and well,—
  "Now you try, Uncle Brown."

Peletiah had the palsy so he shook
  From foot to crown;
The bullet sped, he shook just right,
  And brought the turkey down.

Peletiah left a wife,
  The oldest one in town,
She called the children "duckies dear,"
  They called her "Ducky Brown."

She lived where Moses Mildram lives,
  Was ninety odd years old,
Complacency prolonged her days,
  So I have been told.

Her daughter, Mrs. Preston,
  Who died a few years later,
Was remarkable for kindliness,
  So gentle was her nature.

Ye petulent and peevish wives,
  Who would grow old respected,
Wear in your hearts the sunny smiles,
  That often are neglected.

THE BROTHERS KIMBALL.

Edmond Kimball and his brother Nat,
  Who years ago were gathered to their kin,
Whose early days were spent upon the sea,

Well known to us as true and worthy men.
Old Uncle Nat was called a miser, why?
He had no pride, and cared still less for food,
He sought not fame—his wants indeed were few;
If he ambition had, 'twas that he might be good;
He had a strong and natural love for place,
The house, the barn, each rock, the hollow tree,
And all surroundings, were to his heart most dear:
All innovations on his place he could not bear to see.
His old wool hat he'd worn for twenty years,
Had it been lost, would move his heart to tears,
As though he'd lost a friend; its faded rim,
Its greasy band and crown, were dear to him.
His very pants besmeared with ancient fat,
With buttons odd, were older than his hat;
His cowhide shoes, his long and faded vest,
Well suited *him*; what cared he how *he* dressed.
His market wagon in which he used to ride
To Salem, with rotten seat all settled down one side,
To sell produce, and milk from bruised cans,
That had stood for days in blackest pans.
Once when he was in Salem town,
Without his wagon, walking round,
Some folks took pity on the man,
And put some money in his hand;
He never told them, no not he,
That he held wealth enough in fee,
But held his feeble hand and took it,
And gladly put it in his pocket.
This may or it may not be true,
'Twas told to me as I tell you.
Small his bump of order was,
He had no systematic laws;
The debris all about his house,
Rotten carts, and sleighs, and ploughs,
Old harnesses and broken hames,

(3)

Yokes and saddles, rusty chains,
And even the decaying fences
Were suffered thus, to save expenses;
With rotton shingles, boards and planks,
While he had thousands in the banks;
While pigs invade the kitchen floor,
And cows were dunging round the door;
The house and barn had many a rat,
Was full a match for any cat;
Into the house the chickens comes,
Hunt all about to find the crumbs,
And e're they leave, drop their——excresence.
In such a home, on such a place,
Nathaniel Kimball spent his days;
His well worn Bible—Holy word!
Shows how Nathaniel feared the Lord;
The even tenor of his ways,
Prolonged his life for ripe old age;
He was contented with his lot;
Was he a miser?   Was he not?
It to his credit should be said,
He'd give half as much as brother Ed;
"I am half as rich said Uncle Nat,
As brother Edmund." "Go and see,"
And bring the paper back to me.
He hoped for life among the blest;
At ninety he went to rest.
Many have sneered 'bout Uncle Nat,
Who never paid their honest debts.

TOWN LOCALITIES.

Wenham is a curious place,
    With many a curious name;
There's Wenham lake where ice is cut,
    Which has a world-wide fame.

Devil's Hollow where the witches dwell;
  The Causway and West End,
And Egypt, and the Giant's grove,
  West of the lake extend.

Pleasant, Mud, and Cedar ponds,
  And the lake all in a row,
Three thousand acres in a swamp,
  Lie northwest you know.

Ashbury grove and Dodges row,
  And also Wenham Neck,
Little Comfort, Israel's shore,
  What more can one expect?

There's a town with local names,
  A half a score or more,
Which indicate a set of facts,
  Were never known before.

Egyptians there may cut the ice,
  Send it to England's Queen,
Within a mile of Dismal Swamp,
  A wood of endless green.

Should sickness, death or poverty
  Cause us grief or ill,
I do not think we should repine,—
  We've a Little Comfort still.

Our town has always famous been
For giving titles unto men;
There's Capt. This and Capt. That,
And Captains all around,—
A stranger might be led to think
That half the men in town
Had held commissions in their day,
If unacquainted with our way.
There's 'Squire Kimball, 'Squire Thorn,

Master Conant, Master John,
Master Stephen, Master 'Miah,
Uncle Peter, Uncle 'Ziah,
Uncle Josh, Ned and Nat,
The Devil next,—and what of that ?—
Colonel Porter, Colonel Kent,
Then comes the deacons and then the aunts.
Deacon Nichols, Deacon Patch,
Jacob Dodge and Foster and Deacon Kimball,
Bless my soul! I'd sooner read a roster!
Aunt Ducky, Aunt Thorn, and a score of others.
Here's lots of Uncles, lots of Aunts,
But where in creation are all the brothers ?
All this is very sociable,
For one I've no objections,
Were all these uncles and these aunts
Real bonafide connexions.

But titles often are bestowed
For purposes of fun ;
With Masters, Colonels, Captains, Aunts,
And Deacons I've now done.

STRAYED OR STOLEN.

Some years ago I heard there was
A great excitement about a horse ;
Some thief had broken into the barn
And stole a horse and rode from town.
"How could the rascal have the heart
To steal him from my butcher's cart ?
That horse was mine, it was'nt his'n
If I catch the rogue he'l go to prison.
But all this time the donkey was—
'I'll straight to Salem, yes I will,
And advertise it in a bill ;
I'll have them stuck up all around,

On every fence in every town.
And I will give a great reward,
To have the horse to me restored.
I am amazed beyond belief ;
What a bold and daring thief !
     But all this time the donkey was—
     With paste and bottle in his hand,
     In Essex there appeared a man ;
     On the fence he rubbed a brush,
     Spread o'er the board a sticky mush,
     And over that he spread a bill.
     Strayed or stolen, (if you will,)
     And thus he went all through the town,
     Posting handbills all around.
     But all this time his donkey was—
In Ipswich there appeared a man,
A lot of posters in his hand ;
Which told about the Wenham theft,
How a thief with horse had left ;
On the handbill it was said,
The color of the horse was red ;
Who ever will this horse restore,
Shall have ten dollars, if not more.
But all this time the donkey was—
In Topsfield and in Danvers too,
These bills were posted up to view.
In Beverly and Middleton,
On many a fence and post and stone,
"Strayed or stolen", might be read,
How an honest butcher had
His horse all stolen in the night,
And trotted off ere morning light.
But all this time—
     For days no tidings did he hear
     About the creature far or near.
     Grieved at the loss, expense, and bother,

He thought he'd better buy another.
"How unlucky on the whole
To own a horse and have him stole,
All advertising is in vain ;
I'll never see my horse again !"
But the starving creature *all this time*—
One morn while rattling in the hay,
He *thought* he heard a horse's neigh ;
"'Tis force of habit that is all,
Lord ! how I miss him from the stall !"
So pitching down a little hay,
He fed his cow and went away.
When in the house, he told his wife
He'd heard a horse as real as life.
The poor old donkey, *where was he?*
"It can't be possible, thought he—
I'll go this minute, look and see:"
He cast beneath the barn his eyes :
The man and horse both looked surprised.
"You tarnal beast, how came you here ?
I've hunted for you far and near."
The creature whinnied,—seemed to say
"Just please to fetch me down some hay."
The people joke the man this day,
About the horse 't was stolen away.

A Remarkable Dream.

As I sat in my easy chair,
    'Twas in my cottage home.
My cheerful wife had gone to bed,
    And I was all alone.

I had been reading in a book
    Munchausen wrote of old;
Some lies the most remarkable
    That ever have been told.

The muses danced before my eyes,
  Which I in sleep had closed;
A vision rare I did behold,
  While in my chair I dozed.

I saw some men dig round a rock,
  They made it free and loose;
They had the debris cleared away,
  And raised it up with screws.

All, all the voters in the town
  Were working on a lane;
Which led from where the rock was dug,
  Unto the village plain.

Some carpenters I saw at work
  Upon a mighty sled;
Why build it of such heavy oak?
  To haul the rock they said.

For gracious sake! what does it weigh?
  A hundred tons or so;
We mean to draw it on this sled
  In winter on the snow.

And have it placed upon the green,
  Inside the oval lot ;
'T will make a noble monument
  As any town has got.

Anon I thought the scene was changed,
  'T was winter cold and drear;
And yokes of oxen coming in
  To town from everywhere.

The rock was loaded on the sled,
  'T was nearly eight feet high;
A heavy cable from a ship
  Was laying handy by.

The chain was hooked unto the sled,

The oxen to the chain,
And such a shouting, "Star, come up,"
  I ne'er shall hear again.

A multitude of people had
  Come in from neighboring towns;
Gentlemen with ladies fair,
  And many rustic clowns.

That ponderous rock began to move;
  The sled to glide along,
Mid waving of the handkerchief,
The shouting of the throng.

The sled drew up before the church,
  The teams stretched all along;
The hindermost oxen on the mall,
  The foremost at the pond.

The blue frocks all went to the hall,
  And there they had a lunch,
A hundred teamsters whips in hand
  All eating in a bunch.

Again I thought the scene had changed
  I felt the summer breeze;
Insects buzzing in the air,
  And birds sang in the trees.

The cooling zephyrs wafted on
  The flowers sweet perfume;
A multitude was gathered round,
  All happy I presume.

The rock was placed upon its bed
  Two feet above the ground;
For a foundation had been built,
  Of big rocks placed around.

I said 'twas placed upon its bed,
  But yet it was not quite;

Some crippled soldiers waited to
    Perform a little rite.

A band with music on a form,
    Filled all the space around;
Playing a requiem for the dead,
    With low, melodious sound.

O could the spirits of the dead,
    Once hear that martial strain,
They would come forth from southern graves
  , And be with us again.

Just then a bustle in the crowd,
    Which my attention drew;
A score of men came on the stand,
    Arrayed in army-blue.

The excitement soon became intense,
    The dead alive again;
O, such a rushing as there was
    no take them by the hand.

There was Evans, Clark, and Charley Dodge,
Two Dudleys, and my brother Dan;
Young Merrill, Irvine Smith,
Thomas Turney, every man
Who went to war and lost his life.
The brothers Tuttle from the Neck,
Ben Ingersol and William Beck;
Henry Homan, Daniel Shea,
All those and more I say.
One Peter and one William Dodge,
Page, Quimby, and Charles Henderson;
Fred Howland, Dennis Sullivan,
And several whom I never knew,
Who fairly seemed to stand in view.
The people shout for very joy;
Such happiness without alloy—

(4)

Women fainted at the sight
For very ecstacy—Beholding their friends again.
The cannon roar, the bell struck up a merry peal;
The band sweetly played "Lang Syne"
And at the last refrain the spirits vanished.
Then I heard my name called.
With diffidence I did reply,
"Why call on me ? there's
Greater here than I !"
I stood upon the stand. Those spirits fled,
And the souls of our honored dead,
Their dear remains whom we knew in life,
In sickness died, or fell in battle strife.
At Fredericksburg, where Burnside fought in vain,
Young Dudley fell among the thousand slain ;
While in a boat a bullet from the town
Struck his young life—he fell, he sank, and drowned.
Peter and William Dodge both were shot and fell
Mid leaden hail, the screams of bursting shell,
The noisy drums, the heavy cannon's roar :
And heroes lay dying in their gore.
In Florida, Charles Henderson was shot.
Addison Center the typhoid fever got.
Henry Homer by accident unto his death he came
Thomas Turner was shot and died the same.
Fever and consumption caused the death of Beck.
The brothers Tuttle who went from Wenham Neck
Were shot in war ; the fate of others never will be known
There has no record unto me been shown.
The fate of Ingersoll and my brother Dan,
Transcends in cruelty all the art of man ;
In a loathsome prison they starved and pined and died ;
Where the blood of thousands unto heaven cried.
God heard their cry, and in wrath decreed
That cursed rebellion never should succeed.
I' d gone thus far with my rhyming talk

When a Magician struck the noble rock;
Lo! there burst forth in bright and yellow flames
In burning light, all our heroes' names.

A pavillon had been built upon the village green,
Our wives and daughters mixed in the busy scene
With baskets on their arms, all gaily dressed,
Preparing a dinner for a thousand guest.
A long procession formed in proud array;
It was July the 4th our happy natal day.
They marched with music's martial strain,
And I myself was moving in the train.
How splendidly the tables had been spread
With evergreens and garlands overhead;
With pots of flowers at intervals along,
And rich abundance to feast the happy throng;
We had all marched in, and each had found a place
And reverentially bowed, while a man of God said Grace.
Then all fell to eating, and I had filled my plate
With some dainty bits,—when my wife shook me by the
shoulders, "Are you going to sleep in that chair all night?
Here it is one o'clock." When lo! all this celebration was
but a dream; but would to Heaven it had been true, for
such a monument would be a credit to the town. And here
you see I lost a good dinner.

A few more words and then, adieu;
My poem I have read it through,
The local matter has amused,
And many names I've freely used.
If any body is offended,
I beg your pardon, t'want intended;
. Many things I *might* have said,
About the follies of the dead,
But all in all I am inclined
To treat the past with feelings kind.
We have no cause to feel ashamed,
Our ancestors had wit and fame;

Virtues speak with modest voice,
But folly always makes a noise.

FINIS.

OLD MILAN.

My friends, I promised in my bill,
  To speak of Danvers men;
This promise I will now fulfil,
  On whom shall I begin.

A negro fifty years ago,
  Was living in this place, (Putnam plains)
He was a jolly African,
  Fair sample of his race.

Everybody then sold rum,
  Who kept a grocery store;
Most persons took their daily glass,
  On holidays drank more.

Danvers always had its ways,
  Always fond of fun;
Ever ready for a dupe,
  To play some trick upon.

Eben Berry's father, kept
  A cross and vicious ram;
And Milan butted like a sheep,
  When he had had a dram.

The wags pretended for a bet,
  Was laid upon his head;
That he could butt old Berry's ram,
  And knock the creature dead.

Accordingly the day was set,
  And bets were running high,
And a crowd of tricky men,

Were gathered standing by.

They brought the ram into the ring,
    And placed them head and head;
The owner said that he much feared
    His ram would soon be dead.

Down went Milan on his knees.
    And shook his woolly pate;
The mutton surely seemed to think
    He'd got a worthy mate.

The sheep he trotted on all four,
    The nigger did the same;
Down dropped old Milan by the blow,
    The loser in the game.

THE DANVERS MEN AND THE DANVERS POEM.

I speak as a Phrenologist and shall that freedom take,
To criticize the minds of men and observations make;
You paid me once for doing this, you therefore can't complain,
If in the shape of poetry, I do it o'er again.
I have so many in my mind, on whom shall I begin?
Suppose I tackle Deacon X, say he can wield a sledge;
And he can wield a *bargain*, too, a dollar I will wage.
I traded with that deacon once, and guess I ought to know;
The blacksmith got the weather-guage, that will forever do.
I was not in the brotherhood; a heretic by fame!
I disbelieved in Bible truth, and bore a wicked name.
The heathen must the gospel have, and sinners such as I
Must foot the bill in every trade; must I tell you why?
Does not the Bible teach us that the servants of the Lord
Are the stewards of the world, and only they can hoard
Up wealth against the day of need; then here's to cheating
    all we can
All other sects except my own. We'll over-reach our fellow
    man,
And lend a little to the Lord, and keep the rest ourselves.

The Israelites when they left the land of Pharaoh,
Borrowed jewelry and such-like to take with them when
    they go
Unto the land of Canaan.   With *one* talent we must secure
Bliss; must make our calling and election sure.

A contrast now, another man we'll view,
Who every day is seen and known by you;
Whose bilious blood will seldom let him smile,
And when he does, 'tis really worth your while
To see him; but when he does it comes up from his heart,
Like a genial ray of sunshine, but quickly will again depart
To whence it came his sober look will impress the young
    with awe,
He's just the man, true servant of the law,
His courage cool, courteous and discreet,
No braggart he, will any danger meet,
Honest and trusty, reserved and taciturn,
Pump him for a secret you'l never learn,
From him, what you never ought to know,
Cautious and guarded, deliberate and slow,
He is just the man to fill a sheriff's place,
Keep Adams their you'l never fear disgrace.
Now—No. three you know him very well,
Just touch him off with politics he'l fire shot and shell,
He cannot keep a secret, he dearly loves to blow,
You let him know a private fault, and all the world will
    know,
He's quite ambitious in his way, tis oddly manifest,
He is so fond of money, that he goes poorly dressed,
Very prone to argument, will bluntly speak his mind,
And when offended often is abusively inclined,
My dictionary tells me that a blackguard is a man,
Whose language is most foul, who always when he can,
Will sacrifice his friend to perpetrate a joke,
He's tried to gain distinction and has surely won renown,

And everybody hateth him who knows him in the town.
He has a mess of knowledge well stored in his brain,
And wants to tell folks all he knows, he is so proud and
    vain;
I'll close this sketch but must not tell to you this per-
    sons name,
I doubt me, were the tables turned he would have done the
    same.
One thing however I will say which seems to take his part,
His vices are upon his tongue his virtues in his heart.

No. 4.   Your clerks and storekeepers next will my atten-
    tion gain,
Politeness, affability they all have in the main.
Some exceptions I must own and that with much regret,
It never pays to keep a clerk who will pout and fret,
Because the customers can't decide exactly what to buy,
Or doubt about the quality, or deem the price too high.
Everybody has their wants, some greater and some less,
Don't be obsequious unto one because of better dress;
And when a person happens in who looketh like a clown,
Up goes the hair upon his lip his sneering nose come down.
True gentlemen will never think they have especial right,
To treat one with great reverence another with a slight;
Nature quite impartial is the great, the good, the wise,
Find comfort in their virtues, and in mental exercise.
The fool who has but little sense, stored in his little pate,
Derives his chiefest happiness from silly self-conceit;
Be not pompous, be not vain, be affable to all,
And those who've traded with you once—another time will
    call.

No. 5.   There lives near here another man, and he's a man
    of note,
He's witty— can a story tell, and also crack a joke;
When a bit of gossip gets slyly floating round,
It never losses interest by passing Samuel Brown.

He's very shrewd, and very sharp, where bargains can be
    made.
Spreading mortar and soft soap is this person's trade,
Go ask him if he'll plaster, or lay for you some bricks!
He'll snuff all round to smell the cash,—that's one of his tricks;
I'm very busy quoth the man, I have so much to do!
Better get some other one to do the work for you,
I'll pay the money for the job as soon as it is done;
The case is altered dont you see? I rather guess I'll come.
Good natured, keen, and selfish, and very fond of fun,
When once he gets to laughing, thinks he never shall be done.
Insinuating is his style; ingenious is his wit,
He'll talk all round a matter and still not mention it!
Just as a cat attempts to steal,—take a circuit round,
So carefully insinuated, aint that like Samuel Brown?
I love to hear that person talk, his manner is so queer,
No matter how he seems to preach, there's motive in the rear;
His risibilities are great, and by a master stroke,
He'll set his hearers in a laugh at any little joke.
Now Mr. Brown if you are here you'd better not deny it,
Everybody knows it's true, so 'tis no use to try it.
    No. 6. Now I'll mention No. 6, a worthy friend of mine,
He is good natured, sleek and fat, and dresses rather fine,
He's got a little wealth, he feels a little vain,
Has been in several offices, and auctioneers for gain.
He says: Professor how do do? and takes me by the hand,
And pompously will introduce me to another man,
This is Professor Peabody, perhaps you do not know,
This is the great phrenologist; Professor ain't it so?
His self-esteem so lifts him up, and makes him feel superior,
Thus oft he treats his equals, as though they were inferiors;
He has a little friendship, and of gas a little more,
His ostentatious patronage is to his friends a bore;
Maugre all this, I must confess I really like the man,
So smoothly he can wheedle—so artful and so bland.
His consciousness is small, I've often told him so,

One cannot anger him, because his temper is so slow;
His love for approbation, I know is very small,
No envy rankles in his heart; No jealousy at all.
He wishes *everybody* well, his kindness tends that way,
'Tis more in wishes than in deeds, I've heard some people
say,
This crafty man, doth understand, human nature well,
And every trade John A. has made, has made his coffers
swell.
Now I have done with my friend John, so I will say no more,
Except to say, this goes to pay up many an old score;
Now listen all aspiring men, who would grow proud and
grand,
Keep every cent that you can get, get every cent you can.
Shake everybody by the hand, wear a deceitful smile,
Show hypocritical respect, and cheat them all the while:
Wear in your head an oily tongue, don't scruple when you
lie,
Pat everybody on the back, grow old and rich, and die.

No. 7 is a tall diamond in the rough,
I shall describe him; then you will know the person well
enough;
He's been a poet in his day, or written many rhymes,
And funny things he's had to say in verse at various times.
Eben Berry knows that man, and so does Mason Brown;
There was a poem written once and peddled through th' town.
The friendship of a man who lives by others dying,
Creates suspicion in my mind, in such I've no relying;
His advertisement does not say, I'm pleased to find you
married,
But says in substance, please to die I'll gladly see you buried.
'Tis said that surgeons do rejoice when people break their
bones,
And lawyers rub their hands in glee when heads are broke
with stones.

Broken bargains, broken heads, bring in the lawyer's fees,
Broken arms and broken legs will the surgeons please;
The surgeon and the lawyer and the undertaker these,
Live by our aches and broken limbs, and lastly our decease.
Then Peter Wyatt, and Dr. Chase, and Squire H. L. Hadley,
Should like freemasons all shake hands in close fraternity.
No. 8.   Captain P. reputed rich twenty years ago,
If twenty thousand dollars, maketh anybody so;
By southern men he lost it all. by trusting them with shoes,
And this misfortune brought upon him much unjust abuse;
Were he now rich he might be proud, the poor treat with
      contempt;
We see the man as God ordained from vanity exempt.
He who bears adversity resigned to Heaven's will.
Eben Putnam though he's poor, I can respect him still;
Ye rich and wealthy who are raised above temptations snare,
Who never felt the trying needs of hunger, strife and care,
Who oft' mistakingly suppose you are much better born,
Who treat the accidents and faults of poverty with scorn.
Consider well, and ask yourself what might have been your lot,
Had *you* been poor, and had temptation entered at your gate?
Then treat the poor with kind respect, it justly is their due,
'Twill stifle envy in their hearts, and win respect for you,
'Tis lack of kindness and respect that doom the poor to
      crime,
Pride mortified the want of bread in these hard, idle times.

    1861.   The guns of Sumpter shook the continent!
Foul treason gnashed its bloody teeth,
To crush the soul of liberty; Secession
Denied the boon by patriots bequeathed
To all the sons of freedom, law, and right,
To conquer justice by the sword and might,
One who ruled by the people's choice,
Did stamp the earth and raise his potent voice.
When lo! a million of heroes from the earth,

Came up in mart.al array, marched forth
To crush the reptile, treason, 'neath their honest feet,
Natives and the sons of Erin meet.
The shamrock from the island green,
The starry banner both in battle seen,
Our hills gave birth to cannon ready east,
The eagle waved from every pole and mast.
Union and liberty became the battle cry,
The dearest words to heroes when they die;
Four thousand miles of country in a flame,
Rising to arms from Mexico to Maine,
What history can afford a tale like this,
To *die for freedom* was our soldiers bliss.
On many a bloody field there bled and died,
The alien and the yankee side by side,
O where are those whom shortly since we knew,
Thy martyrs fell, in glory passed from view.
Their bones are mouldering beneath a Southern sod;
In heaven, I trust, they're dwelling with their God.
'Mid clash of arms, they wrote their wills in gore,
Bequeathing Liberty and Union evermore.
Eighty from Danvers, this old historic town,
Have bled and died, preserving its renown.
Haste ye the monument that shall preserve the fame
Of those who fell to save your honored name.
Proud am I of this. my native place,
For never yet has Danvers borne disgrace.

CPSIA information can be obtained
at www.ICGtesting.com
Printed in the USA
BVHW070811040219
539400BV00034B/2702/P